FUNNY JOKES

FOR

YEAR OLD KIDS

HUNDREDS OF HILARIOUS JOKES INSIDE!

JIMMY JONES

Hundreds of really funny, hilarious jokes that will have the kids in fits of laughter in no time!

They're all in here - the funniest
- Jokes
- Riddles
- Tongue Twisters
- Knock Knock Jokes

for 7 year old kids!

Funny kids love funny jokes and this brand new collection of original and classic jokes promises hours of fun for the whole family!

Books by Jimmy Jones

Funny Jokes For Funny Kids
Knock Knock Jokes For Funny Kids

Funny Jokes For Kids Series
All Ages 5 -12!

To see all the latest books by
Jimmy Jones just go to
kidsjokebooks.com

Contents

Funny Jokes!

Why did the snowman wear a bow tie?
To go to the snowball!

How do ghosts get their mail?
From the ghost office!

What sort of dog really loves bubble baths?
Shampoodles!

Why did the astronaut leave the crowded room?

He needed some space!

What do cats eat for desert?

Mice cream!

What sound does a chicken's phone make?

Wing Wing!

What did the cloud wear underneath his raincoat?

Thunderpants!

What do you call a boy stuck to a wall?

Art!

What time do ducks wake up?

The quack of dawn!

How did the fish get to work?
He hailed a crab!

What did the fairy use to clean her teeth?
Fairy Floss!

Why are beavers always on the internet?
They never log off!

Where is the witch's garage?
The broom closet!

What is 188 feet tall and made from cheese and pepperoni?
The leaning tower of Pizza!

What game to mice play?
Hide and squeak!

What do elves love learning the most at school?

The elf-abet!

Why was the baker a millionaire?

He made heaps of dough!

What did cavemen use to cut down trees?

A dino-saw!

How can you cut a wave in half?
With a sea saw!

What instrument can dogs play?
The Trom-Bone!

What do you call an elephant in your refrigerator?
Stuck!

Why is it so expensive to have pet pelicans?
You get huge bills!

What is the easiest way to count 273 cows?
Use a cowculator!

Which word is always spelt wrong?
Wrong!

What do you call a boy with really short hair?

Shawn!

When is the best time to buy a bird?

When they are going cheep!

What do you call a snowman who has been sunbaking for a week?

Water!

What would Superman be called if he lost all his super powers?

Man!

What do you get if you cross a rooster with a poodle?

A CockaPoodleDoo!

Which state has really small cans of soft drink?

Mini Soda!

What do you call a polar bear in the desert?

Lost!

Why can't you see elephants hiding in a tree?

Because they are really good at it!

What did the bee say when he got home from work?

Honey, I'm home!

How can you learn how to make a banana split?

Go to sundae school!

What do cats put in their drinks?

Mice Cubes

Why did the 3 scientists get rid of their doorbell?

So they could win the no-bell prize!

What do you call a boy who is a long way away?

Miles!

What do crabs do on their birthday?

They shell-abrate!

What do you call a man lifting a car with his hands?

Jack

What did the doctor say to the patient who thought he was a dog?

Sit!

Why didn't the bird pay for dinner?

It was too cheep!

How did the barber win the marathon?

He took a shortcut!

Why did the rooster stop crossing the road?
He was too chicken!

What did the doctor do to the patient who had water on the brain?
Gave him a tap on the head!

What roads do ghosts like to haunt?
Dead ends!

What do you get if you cross a skunk with a teddy?

Pooh Bear!

Why did the computer go crazy?

It had a screw loose!

What do you get if you cross a vampire with a teacher?

Lots of blood tests!

What do you call a boy who hits a baseball over the fence?

Homer!

Which piece of a computer is an alien's favorite?

The space bar!

Where did the car go for a morning swim?

The carpool!

Why did the monkey have a day off?
Work was driving him bananas!

What happens if you cross a fish with an elephant?
You get swimming trunks!

What kind of dog did the ghost have?
A boodle!

What do you call a big bodybuilder?
Jim!

What do really short kids do after school?
Their gnome work!

What do you call an auto mechanic?
Axel!

Why did the squirrel keep his secret?
He was a tough nut to crack!

Why do basketball players love babies so much?
Because they both dribble!

What do you get if you cross a toad with a galaxy?
Star Warts!

Why couldn't the astronaut go to the moon?
It was full!

What do you call a really cold dog?
A Pup-Sicle!

What do you get if you cross a boomerang with a christmas present?
A gift that returns itself!

What is a polar bear's favorite snack?
Ice Burgers!

Why was the Egyptian boy so sad?
His dad was a mummy!

What do you call a lady climbing a wall?
Ivy!

What do you call a white bear at the North Pole?

A Polar Brrrrr!

What should you give a pig who has a rash?

Some oinkment!

How can you see a leopard at night?

Use a spotlight!

Which bet has never been won?
The alphabet!

Why did the duck cross the road?
The chicken had the day off!

Why did the computer wear glasses?
To improve it's web sight!

What do you get if you cross a duck with a rooster?

A bird that wakes you up at the

quack of dawn!

Which day do fish hate?

Fryday!

What did Santa do in his vegetable patch?

Hoe, Hoe, Hoe!

What do you call a nervous witch?
A Twitch!

What do you call a lawyer's daughter?
Sue!

What do you get if you cross an alligator with a camera?
A snapshot!

What is the best place for an elephant to store her luggage?

In her trunk!

What do toads play after school?

Leapfrog!

What sound can you hear when a train is eating?

Chew chew!

Why did the flea lose his job?

He wasn't up to scratch

Why doesn't Peter Pan ever stop flying?

He Neverlands!

What do you get if you dive into the Red Sea?

Wet!

If the cheese isn't your cheese, what sort of cheese is it?

Nacho cheese!

What game did the Brontosaurus play with the caveman?

Squash!

Why did the whale get dressed in his best clothes?

He was going to the Orca-stra!

Funny Knock Knock Jokes!

Knock knock.

Who's there?

Heaven.

Heaven who?

Heaven seen you in ages!

You're looking good!

Knock knock.

Who's there?

Cupid.

Cupid who?

Cupid quiet! I'm trying to sleep here!

Knock knock.

Who's there?

Athena.

Athena who?

Athena shooting star last night so I made a wish!

Knock knock.

Who's there?

Who Who.

Who Who Who?

How long have you had a pet owl?

Knock knock.

Who's there?

Iva.

Iva who?

Iva feeling we have met before somewhere!

Knock knock.

Who's there?

Udder.

Udder who?

You look a bit Udder the weather!

Are you sick?

Knock knock.

Who's there?

Sarah.

Sarah who?

Sarah problem with your door because I can't open it!

Knock knock.

Who's there?

Nanna.

Nanna who?

Nanna your business! It's top secret!

Knock knock.

Who's there?

Radio.

Radio who?

Radio not, I'm coming in!

Knock knock.

Who's there?

Cheese.

Cheese who?

Cheese a very good singer!

Want to see her new band?

Knock knock.

Who's there?

Canoe.

Canoe who?

Canoe help me fix my flat tire?

Knock knock.

Who's there?

Avery.

Avery who?

Avery big storm is coming!

Please let me in!

Knock knock.

Who's there?

Ice cream.

Ice cream who?

Ice cream when I jump in the pool!

It's fun!

Knock knock.

Who's there?

Says.

Says who?

Says me, that's who! Ha Ha!

Knock knock.

Who's there?

Ida.

Ida who?

Ida rather be inside than out here in the rain!

Knock knock.

Who's there?

Will.

Will who?

Will you let me in before I freeze?

Knock knock.

Who's there?

Wanda.

Wanda who?

I Wanda what we can do with all this money my aunt gave me?

Knock knock.

Who's there?

Phil.

Phil who?

Phil the car please, we're low on gas!

Knock knock.

Who's there?

Yeast.

Yeast who?

The yeast you can do is let me in!

I've been waiting for ages!

Knock knock.

Who's there?

Icy.

Icy who?

Icy you through the keyhole!

Please open up!

Knock knock.

Who's there?

Venice.

Venice who?

Venice your dad getting home?

He's late!

Knock knock.

Who's there?

Sancho.

Sancho who?

Sancho an email 2 days ago and you

still haven't replied!

Knock knock.

Who's there?

Gerald.

Gerald who?

It's Gerald friend from school!

Don't you recognize me?

Knock knock.

Who's there?

Owl.

Owl who?

Owl be very happy when you finally

open the door!

Knock knock.

Who's there?

Howl.

Howl who?

Howl you know if you don't ever open up this door!

Knock knock.

Who's there?

Major.

Major who?

Major day with all these jokes, didn't I?

Knock knock.

Who's there?

Omar.

Omar who?

Omar goodness, that food smells delicious!

Knock knock.

Who's there?

Ben.

Ben who?

Ben away for years but now I'm back! Let's party!

Knock knock.

Who's there?

Lionel.

Lionel who?

Lionel bite you if you put your arm in his mouth!

Knock knock.

Who's there?

Water.

Water who?

Water you doing later on today?

Let's play ball in the park!

Knock knock.

Who's there?

Wooden.

Wooden who?

Wooden you like to let me in so I can give you your present?

Knock knock.

Who's there?

Wanda.

Wanda who?

I Wanda come in and use your bathroom!

Knock knock.

Who's there?

Kent.

Kent who?

Kent you see I want to come in?

I've been waiting for 3 hours!

Knock knock.

Who's there?

Rhino.

Rhino who?

Rhino all the funniest knock knock

jokes!

Knock knock.

Who's there?

Sofa.

Sofa who?

Sofa these jokes have been funny!

Here's another one!

Knock knock.

Who's there?

A Tish.

A Tish who?

I think you need to see a doctor!

Knock knock.

Who's there?

Hand.

Hand who?

Hand over your money!

This is a stick up!

Knock knock.

Who's there?

Goose.

Goose who?

Goose who is here for dinner?

Aunt Betty!

Knock knock.

Who's there?

Cook.

Cook who?

Are you a cuckoo clock?

Knock knock.

Who's there?

Aida.

Aida who?

Aida hamburger for lunch and now I'm full!

Knock knock.

Who's there?

Lee.

Lee who?

Lee a key out for me next time and I won't have to knock!

Knock knock.

Who's there?

Arfur.

Arfur who?

Arfur got why I came over!

Knock knock.

Who's there?

Ash.

Ash who?

Bless you! Would you like a tissue?

Knock knock.

Who's there?

Art.

Art who?

r2 d2!

Knock knock.

Who's there?

Meg.

Meg who?

Meg up your mind and let me in!

Knock knock.

Who's there?

Baby owl.

Baby owl who?

Baby owl see you at school next week!

Knock knock.

Who's there?

Bat.

Bat who?

Bat you will never guess who it is!

Knock knock.

Who's there?

Lettuce.

Lettuce who?

Lettuce in please. We are really tired!

Knock knock.

Who's there?

Fanny.

Fanny who?

Fanny body knocks just pretend

you're not home!

Knock knock.

Who's there?

Yukon.

Yukon who?

Yukon say that again!

Knock knock.

Who's there?

Kanye.

Kanye who?

Kanye give me a hand with this parcel? It's really heavy!

Knock knock.

Who's there?

Donna.

Donna who?

Donna want to make a big deal about it but your doorbell is broken!

Knock knock.

Who's there?

Don.

Don who?

Don ya want to open the door before I freeze to death!

Knock knock.

Who's there?

Tennis.

Tennis who?

Tennis five plus five!

I'm good at math!

Knock knock.

Who's there?

Oliver.

Oliver who?

Oliver other kids are busy so can you help me do my chores?

Knock knock.

Who's there?

Avenue.

Avenue who?

Avenue seen the news?

Quick! Let's go!

Knock knock.

Who's there?

A little old lady.

A little old lady who?

I didn't know you went to yodelling school!

Knock knock.

Who's there?

Orange.

Orange who?

Orange you glad I finally made it?

Sorry I'm late!

Knock knock.

Who's there?

Value.

Value who?

Value open the door before this ice cream melts?

Knock knock.

Who's there?

Tyrone.

Tyrone who?

Tyrone shoe laces lazybones!

Funny Riddles!

What side of a bird has the most feathers?
The outside!

What type of dress can never be worn?
Your address!

What asks but never answers?
An owl!

What can you serve but never eat?
A tennis ball!

What is the size of an elephant but weighs nothing?
It's shadow!

What has a bark but doesn't bite?
A tree!

What is dirty after washing?
The bath water!

What has fingers and a thumb but no arm?
A glove!

What stays in the corner but travels the world?
A stamp!

What always hears but never talks?
Your ear!

Where does Friday come before Thursday?
In the dictionary!

What has one eye but cannot see?
A needle!

What allows you to look straight through walls?

A window!

What has 1 head, 4 legs and 1 foot?

A bed!

What do tigers have that no other animal has?

Baby tigers!

A man walked across a lake but didn't get wet.
How?
It was frozen!

What can run but never walk?
Your nose!

Which cheese is made backwards?
Edam!

What is so fragile that saying its name breaks it?

Silence!

What gets wetter the more it dries?

A towel!

What do you have that other people use more than you do?

Your name!

What can run but never walks?
A river!

What is always on the ground but never gets dirty?
Your shadow!

What has keys but no doors?
A piano!

What is at the end of the rainbow?
The letter W!

What tastes better than it smells?
Your tongue!

What do you throw away when you want to use it?
An anchor!

What can you serve but never eat?
A tennis ball!

What never speaks back unless spoken to?
An echo!

What question can never be answered with a yes?
Are you asleep?

How can you spell 'mouse trap' with only 3 letters?

C A T!

Which kind of tree can you carry in your hand?

Palm!

What 2 things can you never eat for breakfast?

Lunch and dinner!

What has hands but can't touch anything?
A clock!

What goes up when water comes down?
An umbrella!

What do you always break before you can use it?
An egg!

Funny

Tongue Twisters!

Tongue Twisters are great fun!
Start off slow.
How fast can you go?

Creepy crabs clammer.
Creepy crabs clammer.
Creepy crabs clammer.

Boat toy boat toy boat toy.
Boat toy boat toy boat toy.
Boat toy boat toy boat toy.

Three fleas flew.
Three fleas flew.
Three fleas flew.

Fry fish freshly.
Fry fish freshly.
Fry fish freshly.

A skunk sat on a stump.
A skunk sat on a stump.
A skunk sat on a stump.

Red letter yellow leather.
Red letter yellow leather.
Red letter yellow leather.

Six thick sticks.
Six thick sticks.
Six thick sticks.

Red boot, blue boot.
Red boot, blue boot.
Red boot, blue boot.

Seven slimy snakes.
Seven slimy snakes.
Seven slimy snakes.

Steve saves stamps.
Steve saves stamps.
Steve saves stamps.

Three free throws.
Three free throws.
Three free throws.

Butter bucket bottom.
Butter bucket bottom.
Butter bucket bottom.

Flash message.
Flash message.
Flash message.

Funny fluffy feathers.
Funny fluffy feathers.
Funny fluffy feathers.

Frogfeet flippers.
Frogfeet flippers.
Frogfeet flippers.

Bill blew blue bubbles.
Bill blew blue bubbles.
Bill blew blue bubbles.

Blue burger burglar.
Blue burger burglar.
Blue burger burglar.

Chip shop chips.
Chip shop chips.
Chip shop chips.

Yellow yo-yos.
Yellow yo-yos.
Yellow yo-yos.

Carol cleans carpets.
Carol cleans carpets.
Carol cleans carpets.

Six sleek swans.
Six sleek swans.
Six sleek swans.

Big blue box of biscuits.
Big blue box of biscuits.
Big blue box of biscuits.

Please place peanuts.
Please place peanuts.
Please place peanuts.

Bonus Funny Jokes!

What do you call a guy with his right arm in a shark's mouth?
Lefty!

Which nails do carpenters try not to hit?
Fingernails!

What do birds send out at Halloween?
Tweets!

What did the doctor say to the patient who thought he was a cat?

How are the kittens?

Why did the farmer drive a steam roller through his field?

He wanted to grow mashed potatoes!

Why did the elephant have her nails painted red?

So she could hide in the strawberry patch!

Which insect can tell the time?
A Clock-roach!

Why did the boy bury his radio?
The batteries were dead!

What has 40 legs but can't walk?
Half a centipede!

What do you call the archaeologist who works for the English Police?

Sherlock Bones!

What did the big raindrop say to the small raindrop?

Two's company but three's a cloud!

What do nuts say if they catch a cold?

Cashew!

What did the astronaut find in his frying pan?

An unidentified frying object!

What happened to the owl that lost his voice?

He just didn't give a hoot!

What do you get if you cross a robber with a chicken?

A peck-pocket!

What do you call a boy floating in the sea with no arms, no legs and no body – just a head?

Bob!

What did the mommy chicken call her baby?

Egg!

How did the engineer find his lost train?

He followed it's tracks!

Why did the man have so much facial hair?
It seemed to just grow on him!

What do you call a mountain climber?
Cliff!

What do you call a dog who has a fever?
A hot dog!

What do you call a thief?
Rob!

Why did the elephant decide to leave the circus?
He was sick and tired of working for peanuts!

What do you call a robber who only steals meat?
A hamburglar!

What do you call a woman with a wooden leg?

Peg!

Why did the frog go to hospital?

To get a hopperation!

Why don't eggs tell jokes?

They might crack up laughing!

What did the doctor say to the patient who snored so much he woke himself up?

Try sleeping in the other room!

What did the Cinderella penguin wear to the ball?

Glass flippers!

What did the farmer call his cow that was twitching and twitching?

Beef Jerky!

Why did the boy wear wet pants?
The label said wash and wear!

Why did Cinderella leave the basketball team?
She always ran away from the ball!

Where does Superman buy his toothpaste?
The supermarket!

When it gets really cold what does an octopus wear?
His coat of arms!

Why did the gorilla have huge nostrils?
She had big fingers!

Why was the fish sad about his report card?
His grades were all under "C"!

Bonus

Knock Knock Jokes!

Knock knock.

Who's there?

Boo.

Boo who?

Don't cry so much, it's not that sad!

Knock knock.

Who's there?

Freddy.

Freddy who?

Freddy or not, here I come!

Knock knock.

Who's there?

Kenya.

Kenya who?

Kenya please hurry up and open this door! It's really cold out here!

Knock knock.

Who's there?

Butter.

Butter who?

I butter tell you some more jokes before you get bored!

Knock knock.

Who's there?

Annie.

Annie who?

Annie idea when this rain will stop?

I'm getting wet!

Knock knock.

Who's there?

Razor.

Razor who?

Razor hands in the air like you just

don't care!

Knock knock.

Who's there?

Tweet.

Tweet who?

Would you like tweet an apple?

They are really tasty!

Knock knock.

Who's there?

Watson.

Watson who?

Watson the tv tonight? I feel like

watching cartoons!

Knock knock.

Who's there?

Iva.

Iva who?

Iva very sore hand from all this knocking!

Knock knock.

Who's there?

Duncan.

Duncan who?

Duncan doughnuts go really well with ice cream!

Knock knock.

Who's there?

Phone.

Phone who?

Phonely I had known you were home

I would have knocked earlier!

Knock knock.

Who's there?

Dozen.

Dozen who?

Dozen all this knocking get a bit

annoying? Ha Ha!

Knock knock.

Who's there?

Avenue.

Avenue who?

Avenue fixed the doorbell yet?

It's still broken!

Knock knock.

Who's there?

Isabel.

Isabel who?

Isabel working yet so I can stop

knocking?

Knock knock.

Who's there?

Sam.

Sam who?

Sam day I will remember my key and then I won't have to knock!

Knock knock.

Who's there?

Snow.

Snow who?

Snow use asking me! I'm 100 years old and can't remember a thing!

Knock knock.

Who's there?

Voodoo.

Voodoo who?

Voodoo you think you are, making me wait so long!

Knock knock.

Who's there?

Iran.

Iran who?

Iran really fast to get here and you're not even ready!

Knock knock.

Who's there?

Isabel.

Isabel who?

I know there Isabel but I like knocking!

Knock knock.

Who's there?

Dishes.

Dishes who?

Dishes the police! Open up!

Knock knock.

Who's there?

Alpaca.

Alpaca who?

Alpaca the suitcase, you pack a the trunk!

Knock knock.

Who's there?

Omar.

Omar who?

Omar goodness I love your shirt! Where did you get it?

Knock knock.

Who's there?

Needle.

Needle who?

Needle hand to move your TV? I've got big muscles!

Knock knock.

Who's there?

Candice.

Candice who?

Candice door open any faster if I push it?

Thank you so much

For reading our book.

I hope you have enjoyed these funny jokes for 7 year old kids as much as my kids and I did as we were putting this book together.

We really had a lot of fun and laughter creating and compiling this book and we really appreciate you for reading our book.

If you could possibly let us know what you thought of our book by way of a review we would really appreciate it 😊

To see all our latest books or leave a review just go to
kidsjokebooks.com
Once again, thanks so much for reading.

All the best,
Jimmy Jones
And also Ella & Alex (the kids)
And even Obi (the dog – he's very cute!)

Made in the USA
Middletown, DE
11 July 2019